The Wacky Life of Dexter

Adam Wafi

ISBN (Paperback): 978-1-7394055-0-2

ISBN (Hardcover): 978-1-7394055-3-3

ISBN (eBook): 978-1-7394055-1-9

Published by Risfa Publishing

Table of Contents

Chapter 1

A zoo. That's probably the best way to describe my house.

"Why is there rabbit poo in the hallway?" my older sister screamed.

"It's cat poo, actually," explained my younger sister.

"I DON'T CARE EVEN IF IT'S DINOSAUR POO. CLEAN THIS UP!"

"Genie, how many times have I told you, no dangerous experiments in the bathroom?" my dad roared.

"Sorry, Dad," said Genie.

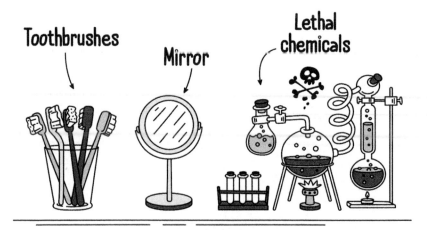

Toothbrushes

Mirror

Lethal chemicals

Our bathroom shelf

"Ouch! Sparta! Why have you left all your sports junk outside my door?" my mom shrieked.

Believe it or not, it was actually quieter than usual that day. Most of my family was already in the kitchen, but no one was talking normally. They were all saying strange things like 'baba,' 'Ani,' and 'bogey'.

"No! We can't let baby Bobby's first word be 'bogey!'"

They were trying to get my baby brother to say his first word, and everyone was competing to be the first person to teach him. I even saw my mom whispering "Mommy, Mommy" in the baby's ear the other day.

My dad saw this and said, "Honey, we agreed that there would be no brainwashing the baby while he's asleep. That's cheating."

We are the Dexters. In total, there are twelve people in the Dexter house.

DAD

MOM

BROTHER

KATHY

MONA

DIYA

SPARTA

FINN and FISHER
(Twins)

(That's me!)

ANI

BOBBY

GENIE

Mom and Dad are the two bosses. Then the three older sisters: Kathy, the therapist; Diya, the DIY sister; and Mona, the money-obsessed sister. Then the three middle brothers: Sparta, the sporty one, and the food and culture-crazy twins, Finn and Fisher.

Then there's me, David Dexter—three words to describe me: small, skinny, and, umm, sensible.

After that, it's my two younger sisters: Genie, the genius, and Ani, the animal lover. Then finally, baby Bobby.

We do have one older brother that left home several years ago. The last time I heard from him, he was somewhere in Asia. I'll tell you about him some other time.

I wasn't in the mood to join in with the baby's first-word competition, as I felt pretty nervous about my first day at Cheapsdale Middle School.

My dad is a professional cook, and breakfast in our house is always a big deal. The table was full of pancakes, pies, treats, and other things, but I didn't feel like having anything too fancy today, so I picked up a piece of toast.

"Oooh, ooh," I heard. The baby looked directly at me, reaching his hands out as though he wanted my toast. The whole family suddenly turned and looked at me.

"The baby wants toast!" screamed Sparta.

"Feed the baby toast!"

One of the twins came rushing over, snatched the toast from my hand, and took it straight to the baby.

"Hey, I was eating that," I grumbled.

The baby soon lost interest. I decided to try a pancake, but it was also snatched out of my hand. In fact, it seemed the baby was only interested in whatever I wanted to eat.

"I'm trying to eat breakfast here," I snapped. My family realized something was wrong.

"You normally never complain," my mum said, sounding worried.

"Maybe you haven't been exercising enough," Sparta chimed in. "Let's have a three-hour weightlifting session when you return from school."

"No, no, I'm fine," I replied.

Genie asked, "Should I do some scans on you to see what's wrong? I'll need to take samples of your poo."

I slowly backed away from Genie. "Uhh... I'm okay, thanks."

"I know what's wrong," interrupted Mona. "Let me guess, you're concerned about the country's financial state and that many of your investments are going down?" Mona was crazy about money and business.

"Mona, I'm ten years old. I don't care about the financial situation of the country."

"What is it?" asked one of the twins while stuffing their faces.

"I'm nervous about this new school," I replied.

"So that was the problem. Just relax. It's just the same as your old school," my mom reassured me.

Sparta said, "It's just ten times bigger with terrifying teachers and ten times more work, ten times worse punishments if you mess up. Oh, and there are also about two thousand students. So, you might get lost or crushed. Or..."

Before he could finish his sentence, two of my sisters shoved croissants in his mouth.

"Don't listen to him," comforted Kathy, the therapist. She began walking toward me, and I knew what was coming. She pulled out her hypnotizing watch and started her routine. "You are calm—you are very, very calm."

"This doesn't work," I muttered.

"WHAT?!" she bellowed.

"I'm calm."

She would get very offended if her hypnotizing procedures didn't work.

"Kathy, please don't hypnotize your siblings at the breakfast table."

"Yes—sorry, Dad."

Soon I headed off, leaving my family trying to program the baby's mind with his first word.

This new school was far away, so I had to leave the house before everyone else. Thankfully, I would not be going alone but with my two friends. As we went to the same elementary school, our parents let us go together. I soon reached Richard's house.

After knocking on Richard's door, he came out immediately with a massive sandwich. Richard really likes his food—you can tell immediately by looking at him.

"How was your holiday?" Richard asked through a mouthful of food.

"Same as usual, nothing special. How about yours?" I asked.

Richard responded, "Well, we had about five weddings and six funerals, and I visited ten different countries for other family events." If you are confused, Richard has a massive family.

Soon we arrived at Isaac's house, and, as usual, he was running late.

"What's taking him so long? I only packed a few sandwiches for the walk to school," complained Richard. I didn't understand how Isaac could be so late for someone who wakes up ridiculously early every day.

Two loud booms were heard from the house, which soon answered our questions.

"Isaac! No explosions in the morning!" we heard his mom shriek.

"Sorry, sorry, sorry. I'm leaving now," Isaac replied.

Soon, Isaac came rushing out of the house with crumpled clothes and black marks on his face. At first glance, you might have thought he could not afford clean clothes or a proper bath. However, it was quite the opposite.

"Change!" his dad yelled while rushing out of the house with cloth and wipes in his hands. He wiped his son's face and fixed up his uniform.

"Please try and make yourself look more presentable for school," he commanded.

"Sorry, Dad."

It seemed like his robot tinkering always ended up with explosions and annoyed neighbors.

"Only two explosions. That's an improvement," Richard commented.

Normal morning at Isaac's house.

"Yes, I'm getting the hang of it," he responded. "It was just a minor setback. But, you see, the CPU system overloaded because the X354 chip couldn't cope with the influx... ."

Richard and I looked at each other. We knew that when he got started, he wouldn't stop. So, we quietly listened to him the rest of the way to school. Honestly, I had no clue what he was talking about, so I nodded and smiled.

We arrived at the new school.

"So, here we are," began Richard dramatically. "Now we become men." We slowly walked toward the door.

"This is middle school. It's not that big of a jump," I said.

"You say that, but before you know it, we'll be growing beards," he replied.

I shook my head as we walked to our new class. We'd been shown around before. I could already see kids with their own small groups, the same as in our old school. We walked past them to find some space to ourselves.

The gossipers, the gamers, the clever kids, the sporty kids, and the bullies. It was not hard to figure out which group I liked the least.

The bullies were made up of three guys: Drake and his two goons, Vincent and Victor. They have been a nightmare since preschool.

Back then, they used to throw diapers at all the children and tried to wipe snot all over our faces. Once they nearly poisoned all of us by putting soap in our food. It was a good thing the teachers realized this just in time.

The entire class made many complaints, and things improved eventually. As we walked past them, the muttering began. It felt like they were plotting something quite unpleasant.

"I've got a bad feeling about this," whimpered Isaac.

"Don't worry. If they try anything, we'll tell the teacher straight away, just like last time," I reassured Isaac.

"It won't be that easy this time," murmured Richard.

"What do you mean?"

"I've heard rumors about the new teaching assistant. Unfortunately, I don't think he will be on our side," Richard replied ominously. Then, as Richard continued to scare us, a paper ball landed on Isaac's desk.

"Looks like you're the first to get a gift from Elder this year," I observed.

The three of us looked back into the corner of the room, where a boy with long black hair sat alone. Although he was usually very quiet, he was the best person to go to for advice. Throughout the year, he'd randomly throw paper balls to people in the class, offering advice, eventually earning the nickname 'Elder'. Even Drake did not try to annoy him.

Gambo, the gamer boy, sitting in front of us, turned around and boasted, "I was the first one, actually."

"What does yours say?" Isaac asked curiously.

"There are two blessings many people waste, health and free time," Gambo read. "But I don't know why he would give me that."

"Maybe because you spend five hours a day playing video games!" Richard yelled.

Before we could see Isaac's paper, the bell rang, and the teacher and his assistant walked in. They looked like complete opposites.

"Hello, everyone! I'm Mr. Joy."

He did, in fact, look extremely joyful. His clothes were bright and festive, and he had a large smile. He also seemed particularly gentle.

"Hello, class," snapped the assistant.

He didn't look too happy. In fact, his frown showed that he would rather be anywhere else but here.

"My name is Mr. Scowl. I'll be the new assistant teacher."

A few of the children started murmuring with each other.

"He looks... a bit frightening," Isaac whispered to me.

Mr. Scowl darted his beady eyes toward Isaac and immediately pointed at him and five other kids.

"You, you, and you four. Out. Now. You will return in ten minutes," Mr. Scowl demanded.

It looked like Mr. Joy wanted to stop Mr. Scowl but was perhaps a bit scared to do so. I had a bad feeling about this assistant teacher. Mr. Joy then made two big announcements.

"Now, as you know, club participation is a big part of this school. Mr. Scowl will be handing out the list of clubs. We'd like you to attend as many as possible. Mr. Scowl, could you please hand out the club list?"

Mr. Scowl glared at Mr. Joy, who flinched.

"Actually, Mr. Scowl, if you like, I could hand them out?" Mr. Joy suggested nervously.

"No, I'll do it." Mr. Scowl started placing large boxes on everyone's desks, which were full of sheets of paper.

How are we going to carry these? I wondered.

Mr. Joy continued with his second announcement. "Later in the year, we will have a fantastic school trip. It's, in fact, a tradition that the first years go somewhere amazing. This year, we're going to have a camping trip..." he paused to let the students grumble and complain before finishing with, "... at a theme park!"

The class all cheered!

Maybe this school isn't so bad after all, I thought. Well, that was before our lessons started.

The teachers were a mixed bag. Some were nice, some were monsters, and some didn't know what they were doing.

In the morning, we had our math lesson. "Does anyone know how to solve this?" asked Mr. Matty. We knew he'd been trying to look up the solutions on his laptop for the last twenty minutes.

How not to be a math teacher

Isaac whispered to me, "Is this really the math teacher?"

One of the clever kids jumped up and offered to answer. *Thank goodness we have some smart kids in the class.*

The last lesson of the day was English. The teacher was very overdramatic. He jumped on the table and cried, "Put your passion into your writing. Imagine you're one of the characters. Feel it!"

"All I feel like doing is going home," complained Richard.

That evening, after describing my first day, my parents, especially my dad, seemed enthusiastic about the new clubs.

"Yes, you should enroll in every single club."

I'm not sure he understood there were about sixty clubs to choose from.

I looked to my siblings for help, but they all looked at me with pity.

Mona explained, "Sorry little bro, we all had to go through the same thing."

The other older siblings all nodded in unison.

Sparta added, "Sixty? You only have to join sixty clubs? We had eighty, and Dad made us go to all of them."

I looked at the twins. They were both shaking in fear.

"Dad, no more clubs, please," they muttered in unison, still traumatized by their past.

I was starting to get a bit nervous.

Diya chimed in, "That's nothing. I had about ninety clubs, and Dad wanted me to join clubs outside of school."

Ani added, "Yeah, that's nothing. Dad made me go to two hundred clubs."

"Ani, you're only six, and your school only has three clubs."

After realizing it wouldn't be possible to persuade my dad, I accepted that I would have to attend every club in my school.

So, I spoke to Isaac and Richard the next day about what happened.

"It seems like our parents have all been talking to each other. My parents told me I need to attend at least thirty," Richard complained.

"Mine said forty," said Isaac grumpily.

"Mine said all of them," I concluded, wondering if our parents were trying to have a competition with each other.

Dad's clubs competition

Chapter 2

So, here we were, headed to the first club of the day.

At 8:00 AM, we were already at school with the other students who were clearly here by force.

"Alright, students, now what you've got to do is put the thread through the needle," our sewing teacher instructed us.

Unfortunately, it seemed like he could not really see properly. It also doesn't help that Drake tried to poke people with a needle. By the end of the lesson, we hadn't really done anything apart from getting pricked by Drake and his goons.

Next, at 9:00 AM, was the bird-watching club. Apparently, nobody wanted to attend apart from the three of us. So we stood outside in a tiny hut—in the freezing cold, accompanied by our teacher.

"Sir, aren't we supposed to have binoculars?"

He responded, "Yes, well, the school can't afford them, so we'll just do this," and then he made a binocular shape with his hands.

"You're joking!" replied Richard, clearly appalled.

The three of us all looked at each other, shocked. We sat there for about an hour, and the only things we found were some beetles.

"Well, that was very exciting, wasn't it?" exclaimed the bird-watching teacher.

"But we didn't see any birds," I remarked.

"No, but we saw some beetles. Isn't that fantastic?"

"How often do we actually see birds?" I inquired.

"Well, last year, we found two."

"You found two in one lesson?"

"No, we found two in the whole year," stated the teacher.

"So, throughout the whole year you spent looking, you only found two birds?" I yelped in disbelief.

We looked at each other and decided not to return to this club.

Our morning lesson began. Some classmates were looking at us, wondering why our heads were on the table with twigs sticking out of our clothes. The teacher hadn't arrived yet, and the class monitor walked over to us, arms crossed with a frown.

We called him the class monitor because he behaved like a mini teacher. He was very bossy and strict and basically managed the class since the time we were in preschool.

"You three, this is not the correct way to sit in class. You should keep your backs straight," the class monitor nagged.

When we didn't budge, he slammed his hand on my desk. I stood up in shock and accidentally head-butted the class monitor.

"Sorry, sorry," I said.

"It's fine. I've gotten used to it by now," muttered the class monitor, rubbing his forehead.

Isaac wasn't getting up. "No, I don't want to look at any more birds. I hate bird watching."

At that moment, the science teacher arrived. He seemed to have been involved in several accidents on his way here. His clothes were a complete mess, and he seemed to have some strange slime spread over his face and hair.

The gossip kids whispered, "Apparently, this teacher is a total madman and he is very dangerous."

"Why does the school keep him?"

"Well, you know the principal. He's always trying to save money. Apparently, this teacher works for free."

I was beginning to understand why this place was named Cheapsdale School.

We were quite looking forward to the science lesson. You expect the science experience will get more exciting as you get older. Usually, however, this is a bit of a disappointment.

Expectation: Massive explosions. Reality: Watching an egg float in water.

Egg floating experiment

Fresh water   Salt water

Expectation   **Reality**

Experiments in science class

"Okay, class, today, we will start with the practical. We're going to be working with magnesium. Be careful. Magnesium causes extreme flashes of light," explained the science teacher.

"Could this blind someone?" Drake beamed. He seemed disturbingly excited by the idea.

"Yes, if you use it too much and mix it with the wrong chemicals."

"Excellent," rejoiced Drake. Although Drake's enthusiasm was concerning, I couldn't help but feel excited about this lesson. We split up into groups and began experimenting.

Drake and his friends were told off for trying to get double the amount of every ingredient. They seemed to be trying to compete to see who could make the biggest flash bomb. Soon enough, the experiment began, and the class was full of bright lights.

"Wow! Finally! Something that is actually functioning and exciting in this school," noted Isaac.

While distracted by Isaac's bright light, Drake and one of his friends swapped some of my ingredients while my head was turned.

The experiment was simple: light up the magnesium and make it sparkle brilliantly. We also put some weird liquid on it to prevent it from being too bright.

"Oh, this is going to be brilliant," Drake smirked. He and his friends had stopped working, waiting for the show to start.

It does smell a bit funny, I thought as the chemical reaction started.

It should have started to shine bright white, but mine was blooming in multi-colored rainbows. It was stunningly beautiful.

"You!" The science teacher was red in the face and stormed towards me. I was sure I was going to be in mega trouble, but he came over and patted me on the shoulder.

"Amazing. Absolutely amazing. How did you know adding this chemical would create multi-colored light?"

Accidentally being awesome

"Fantastic! You know what? You don't even have to pack anything away."

Drake and his friends had their mouths wide open in shock.

Drake spat, "How does he always get away with this?"

Finally, it was lunchtime, but we had the rock, paper, scissors club to attend. "No, no, no! I'm not going anywhere," protested Richard. He grabbed onto a goalpost for dear life. "No more clubs. I want to go to lunch!"

"Come on, we'll get in trouble with our parents. We've got to go," I urged, trying to drag him away. I don't know why I bothered. He was twice my size and wasn't moving an inch.

I saw Bolt, one of the sporty kids, walking with his friends toward us. The sporty kids are all massive. It makes you wonder what they're being fed. They seemed several years older than us. Some of them already seemed to be growing facial hair. "Are you boys heading off to the rock, paper, scissors club?" he thundered. I thought he was going to start making fun of us. "Let me guess, your parents forced you as well? We all have to go, too," Bolt said grumpily.

One of the sporty kids grabbed Richard by the arm. "Let's go, Richard." He eventually relented, and off we went. It was terrible. It was literally an hour of playing rock, paper, scissors.

"My arms, my arms," whined Isaac. By the end of it, we were exhausted.

We had rugby (it's like American football) for the second half of lunch. Probably the most painful twenty minutes of my life. It was non-stop tackling and pushing—all to get a ball. I'm not sure if I've told you already, but I'm very small and skinny. I like being small and skinny, but they're probably not the best qualities to be a rugby player.

Drake was in this club. Unfortunately, he was on the opposing team and seemed to be looking forward to tackling me. Thankfully, I'd already thought of a plan.

"Give me the ball!" screamed Drake as he charged straight toward me.

"Sure, here you go," I answered simply and gave the ball directly to him even though he was on the other team.

"Huh. What?" He wasn't expecting that. He stumbled with the ball and fell over.

I picked up the ball and walked toward the goal area.

"It's a tie!" screamed the rugby coach. "Great work, David."

Drake punched the ground in frustration.

Although I wouldn't say I liked this club, one person absolutely loved it: Richard. He would pick up the ball and walk through the entire pitch. Then, no matter who tried to tackle him, he would walk normally as if nobody was there.

I guess that was the benefit of being a giant.

In the afternoon, we had our French lesson. I had never really studied French before, but I always thought French teachers wore funny hats and strange clothes and had a French accent.

The teacher, Mr. Stetson, came in dressed like a cowboy, "Banjo!" he said.

"It's 'bonjour'," one of the clever kids corrected.

I wondered if he had come to the wrong class.

"Now, I don't know much French, so I'll need your help." He said.

What on Earth?

Thankfully, the clever kids helped him, "Say Je m'appelle, Mr. Stetson."

"Je m'appelle, Mr. Stetson," repeated the teacher.

"Good, great work," praised Albert. Albert was one of the smartest boys in the class, second only to the class monitor himself. Seeing a teacher being taught by a student was a strange sight.

It looks like the class monitor was about to go insane. "What kind of teacher is this?" he growled as he snapped his pencil in half.

The other kids in the class noticed that the class monitor was about to have a breakdown, and some were getting anxious. This had happened a couple of times in the past—at the other school. The class monitor was extremely strict compared to the teachers, even when we were babies.

Excuse me, teacher, but the diaper-changing time was three minutes ago. You are three minutes late. As an educator, this is unacceptable.

Teacher, this is nowhere near enough homework. This isn't good for children's development. I shall be reporting you to my parents.

Teacher, this work is far too easy. I demand that the class study Shakespeare.

Class monitor through the years

In fact, quite a few of the students looked worried. Even Drake and his friends started to look a bit concerned. Usually, after one of the class monitor's outbursts, things became a bit more difficult in the class.

Everyone in the class turned around to look at me.

"David, hurry up. Go talk to him," urged Bolt. I don't know exactly how this started, but ever since our old school, the whole class expected me to control the class monitor.

I sighed and got up.

"Where do you think you're going?" the teacher queried as he continued his French lesson with the clever kids.

"I just need to tell the class monitor a message about one of the clubs."

"Oh, okay, well the school likes its clubs," the teacher responded. "Maybe I should start a French club."

The clever kids all shouted, "No!"

"Why?" asked Mr. Stetson, looking slightly offended.

"I mean, you're not ready yet, Mr. Stetson. Once you master the language, then you can do the French club. But, for now, you must study," replied Albert.

"Yes, yes. Sorry, I was getting ahead of myself." Mr. Stetson laughed.

I walked over to the class monitor. He looked like he was going to scream at the teacher.

"Hey, class monitor."

"What is it?"

"Are you coming to the class monitor club?"

"What?" He jolted up and squeezed my shoulders in excitement.

"After school today, there's a class monitoring club where we learn how to properly look after a class."

"This is a dream come true!" He looked like he was on the verge of tears. "I suppose dealing with this incompetent teacher can wait a while."

The class seemed to breathe a sigh of relief. I got a thumbs-up from most of my classmates and even a slight nod from Drake, which was nice.

The class monitoring club was not what I expected it to be.

The teacher was wearing an army uniform and made us all line up. "Alright, boys. Do you want to look after your class? Well, you must first learn to look after yourself. Do you understand?"

We all saluted and said, "Sir, yes, sir!"

It felt like we had just joined the army. He made us do all these weird training drills. By the end of it, the class monitor was ecstatic.

"Yes, this is perfect. I must control my class and make sure the students don't get out of hand, and I need the power to do that."

Richard whispered, "David Dexter, you have created a monster."

The next few weeks carried on like this. We went to dozens upon dozens of ridiculous and mostly awful clubs.

I thought we would play something like snap during the card game club, but the school couldn't afford cards. So we had to make our own out of paper.

The checkers club was run by a teacher who didn't know how to play checkers. He actually hated the game!

"This is so boring. Why do we have to play checkers?" the teacher complained.

Then I went to a fruit club. We literally sat there and just stared at the fruit. Eventually, the teacher would describe the fruit.

"Look how green it is. Look at how lovely and rotten it is."

"Why are we using rotten fruit?" someone protested.

"Let me explain. It is a lot cheaper to use the leftovers from the cafeteria. It was the principal's genius idea. An effective way to save money." I was getting increasingly curious about our principal. Our class hadn't seen him yet, but he seemed crazy about saving money.

Isaac seemed to be on the verge of tears, clearly upset at all the useless clubs. "Did you open that piece of paper from Elder?" I asked, thinking that it might comfort him.

"Oh yes, I forgot," he replied, pulling out the ball of paper from his pocket. "With hardship comes ease," he read.

As it turned out, things were about to become easier for Isaac.

It was in the robotics club that we first saw the principal. He was a very tall, skinny man with glasses and an extremely long nose. He had a calculator in one hand and a clipboard in the other.

"It's obvious why the principal is here," said Richard.

"Why?" I asked.

"It's because this is the most expensive and popular club, and he's trying to ensure we don't overspend on it." The principal did look like he was in a lot of pain.

"Today, we will only be learning the theory of robotics. Once you show me that you understand the instructions, then we might start using actual materials," the robotics teacher explained.

We all looked at each other, slightly bored.

"Oh man, I thought we were going to start making things," one of the boys complained.

The teacher started drawing and jotting on the board. Unfortunately, it looked overly complicated with weird coding and equations.

This is going to be even harder than a normal class.

Isaac's hand shot up. "Actually, you've made a mistake there."

He approached the board, rubbed out sections, and re-wrote them.

"Incredible! I didn't think the circuit board could be arranged like this. You are definitely ready to start building," the teacher exclaimed.

"Excuse me, I thought we decided we were going to save materials and not do anything today," moaned the principal.

"That is correct, but this child already completed everything, so we've got no choice." He beamed, clearly thrilled to finally have a student who understood robotics.

"Fine," the principal grumbled as he stormed out of the class.

"Okay, everyone, change of plans. We shall now begin building," exclaimed the teacher.

The class cheered.

We started by making some 'simple' battery-powered cars. Isaac was assisting the teacher and was finally enjoying himself at a club. "Looks like Elder was right, eh?" said Isaac. It was quite fun but very complicated.

"God, help me find a decent club," I uttered.

After a couple of weeks, there was just one last club left for me to attend: the cooking club.

By then, I'd pretty much given up on finding an enjoyable club, and I hate cooking anyway. Unlike me, Isaac and Richard didn't have to come. After arriving, I sat down next to one of the gamer boys, Gambo. He looked miserable.

"Are you okay?" I asked.

"The school has no gaming clubs—none. So what's the world coming to?" Gambo complained.

"I suppose it's hard to make a club where you just play video games."

He put his head in his arms and sobbed, "I'd rather play the demo of Blobberfish 2 than be here."

Since I wasn't able to understand gamer talk, I just patted him on the shoulder.

Soon, a man wearing an enormous chef's hat walked in.

The class was in shock. Even Gambo suddenly sat up straight.

"Oh, my goodness," he gasped.

"What's going on?" I asked.

"Don't you know who that man is? His name is Gusto, one of the best chefs in France. He owns about twenty restaurants. What's he doing here?"

"Hello, everybody," Gusto began in a bored voice with a thick French accent.

"I will be helping with the cooking classes this year to repay an old debt to your principal. However, I must warn you, by the end of the year many of you will not be in this club. But those who survive will be among the world's greatest chefs."

The class looked thrilled.

"Now, we will be starting today with sandwiches."

You could almost see everyone deflating at once. *Sandwiches? How boring.*

Gambo, who had clearly lost interest in the lesson, began telling me about all the games he'd played and reviewed each of them thoroughly. He was basically talking non-stop. Top tip: be incredibly careful with who you sit with in class.

"Yeah, Blockade 4 isn't as good as Blockade 3. They honestly didn't need to update it." I stopped following the recipe because Gambo used most of the ingredients without realizing it.

Mr. Gusto was coming over, so I hastily put together whatever I could see to at least make it look like a sandwich. As he walked past, he judged everyone's sandwiches.

"Poor."

"Terrible."

"Disgusting."

"I will have to shut down this club unless some of you start making something edible." He came over to our desk and looked at my sandwich. "What is this monstrosity?" he barked. My green and slimy sandwich really did look awful.

My slimy but tasty cake

I thought he was going to shout and tell me to leave the club, so I started talking nonsense. Complete nonsense.

"Are you a professional chef judging my sandwich by its cover? Have you no shame? Is this how we judge art, just merely by looks? Are we people of the paintbrush, or is it the taste that is more important?" Finally, my dramatic speech was over. The whole class was staring at me, and I noticed Mr. Gusto was in tears.

"Beautiful, just beautiful. That is indeed what it means to be a great chef."

He took a bite and then exclaimed, "Sacre bleu. This is amazing. So moist and such a unique variety of ingredients. I've changed my mind. It looks like I'm not going to close this place down. Instead, I will turn you all into great chefs." He looked at me in admiration. It looked like this was the one club I wasn't getting out of.

During the afternoon lessons, Richard looked miserable.

"What's up with you?"

Richard cried, "It's my club. They're making me go on a strict healthy diet. I can't take it. I'm not allowed any chocolate or sweets, only once a week. Can you believe that they want me to eat fruits? Fruits!"

That didn't sound too bad, but I'm sure, for Richard, that was probably the end of the world.

Mr. Joy arrived.

"Before starting the lesson, I want to congratulate you on attending so many fantastic clubs."

Mr. Joy walked toward my desk. "I've heard some great things about your cooking Mr. Dexter. It would be lovely to try your sandwiches soon."

Drake was glaring at me.

Chapter 3

After arriving home, I noticed that my family was still trying to persuade my baby brother to say his first word.

"Baby Bobby, say financial stock market," Mona encouraged.

"Why are you teaching him useless words?" stated Diya. "Okay, say ceramic plasterboard."

"Oh yeah, and that's not a useless word," retorted Mona. "When is the baby going to be using ceramic plasterboard?"

The baby's actual name isn't Bobby. His real name was some thirty-letter monstrosity. My parents might have been trying to break the world record for the world's longest baby name. The trouble was that none of us could remember how to say it. So, for now, we were stuck with baby Bobby.

"Okay, come for dinner," my dad called.

We gathered around the table and began chatting away.

"So, how are your clubs going, David?"

"Well, I've been made head chef of the cooking club." The whole family stopped talking, dropped their plates, and gasped.

"Have they gone insane?" asked Sparta.

The twins looked like they were going to be sick.

Kathy, the therapist, asked, "Did you hypnotize them or something?"

"Hey, what do you mean? What's with all these reactions?" I was slightly offended.

"Son, we've seen your cooking in the past," said my mom.

Some of the family members really did look a bit sick now.

"Okay, guys, maybe it didn't look great, but I'm sure it tasted fine," I protested.

"Well, to be fair, we've never actually eaten anything you've made," Mona noted.

Dad, on the other hand, was having the complete opposite reaction. "That's wonderful, son. I'm so proud of you. And, of course, to celebrate, we will have extra cake!"

"To change the topic, I hope you know that one of the most important days of the year is coming up next week," said Sparta.

"What?" I asked.

"Sports day, of course, and I'll be helping out this year, so make sure you come first place in everything."

I had a bad feeling about this.

Soon sports day arrived, and things weren't looking great. The principal had asked Sparta to organize the activities because it was cheaper than paying a professional. As a result, this year's sports day looked more like an army assault course. "This looks too intense for a middle school sports day," Richard complained.

The two times of the year people went to Elder the most were during sports day and during the exam period. I could see him comforting Bolt, who had come second in the sack race. "Look at those below you, so you don't become ungrateful for the blessings you have been given."

There were a lot of families there that day. It is pretty amazing how similar children can be to their parents.

The gaming kids had quite "techy" parents—they were on their phones and they had smartwatches and all sorts of other technical distractions.

The sporty kids had gigantic parents.

The clever kids weren't fans of sports day, and their parents looked like they didn't want to be there either. Usually, they seemed pretty boastful because their children were geniuses, but not today.

Drake's parents were like Drake. They looked terrifying.

Anyway, the event started. Most jump ropes in sixty seconds, tug of war, stilts, heaving sandbags, but—for some weird reason—all my equipment was defective. In fact, nearly everything was broken.

"What on Earth is going on?" demanded Isaac.

One of the gossip kids nudged me. "I think you should go round the back and look at the sports shed. You will find your answers there."

My brother was passing out equipment, and Drake and his friends were with him for some reason.

"Thanks, guys, you've been a great help today," said Sparta.

"Oh, no worries at all," said Drake very politely, which was unlike him.

"I'm glad my brother has such good classmates," Sparta beamed.

"Oh yes. We really do like David," Drake lied.

As Sparta walked away, we could see Drake and his friends breaking apart the equipment slightly.

"You cheats," Richard whispered.

"We've got to do something," Isaac fumed.

We approached my brother. He looked at me but clearly wasn't in a very good mood today because I had lost most of the events. "The boys who were helping you are breaking and sabotaging the equipment."

Sparta responded, "Please don't make excuses. Just try your best for the last race."

"Wow! He walked off," Isaac remarked, stating the obvious.

"Your brother is usually an alright guy. What's up with him?" asked Richard.

"It's just that this is important to him. I feel quite guilty."

"It's not your fault," Richard consoled. "Let's just try to do well in this last race."

The last race was a piggyback race with obstacles.

"We will now be taking a ninety-minute break. Please visit our refreshments area to buy food and drinks. The final race of the day will begin after the break!" came the announcement.

The principal loved sports day. It was an easy way to make money as the parents must pay a small fee to come in. My brother was in the crowds and looked quite gloomy. Richard, my partner, was going to carry me. He'd probably break my back if I tried to carry him.

"Do you think you can win this race, Richard?" I asked.

"No," he responded, "I've got no motivation. I'm too tired. I've been eating too many vegetables. I'm sure it's bad for you to have this much fruit and vegetables in your body."

Although Richard was talking nonsense, it did give me an idea. The thing Richard lacked was motivation. Mr. Gusto, the cooking teacher, was in the stands and didn't look so happy to be there either. Understandably, he wasn't a fan of sports days. I ran over to him, and he immediately cheered up when he saw me.

"Can you do something for me?" I asked. "If you do, I can introduce you to my dad. He's also a professional chef."

"Sacre bleu!" he exclaimed in response. "What a privilege to meet the father of such a fine young cook! What would you like me to do?"

"Make a cake, the biggest one you can make, within the next hour."

An hour later, the principal announced, "Today, as a special treat, there will be a cake at the end of the race for the winning duo, baked by the prestigious Mr. Gusto."

We saw a massive cake at the end of the finish line, where the trophy was. Although most of the crowd looked really amazed by it, Richard looked like he had turned into a zombie. He was drooling while repeating, "Cake, cake, cake." Then he turned to me. "Alright, we must win this."

I'd never seen him this motivated before.

Isaac pointed out, "Statistically, that is very unlikely. The fastest runners are here, and I'm sure Drake is up to something."

"I don't care about the statistics. Are we boys, or are we men? We will race them on the beaches and in the streets. We shall never surrender." He gave quite a spectacular speech. It's incredible what a cake can do to a person.

Not only was this a piggyback race, but there were numerous obstacles to overcome. There were heavy sandbags, vertical poles, and barrels we had to roll, to name a few. Sparta's crazy race and Drake's sabotaging meant that this course would be a nightmare. Soon the race began.

"On your marks, get set, go!"

Immediately after setting off, several people fell over, and Drake was muttering near us, "Hah, worked like a charm."

I didn't want to look back to see what had happened. Plus, it's hard to look back while you're riding on the back of another person.

Richard stepped on some slime that had been laid on the track, and we fell over like the rest. Drake looked back at us and laughed.

To my surprise, Richard picked me back up, despite being covered in this strange slime, and started blitzing through the rest of the obstacles. The crowd was amazed. But Drake still had a massive lead and was confident he would win.

I whispered to Richard, "I really don't think we're going to get any cake at this rate."

Would you believe it? He went even faster! We were close to the finish line, but Drake was closer. Before I knew it, we'd caught up with Drake and began overtaking him. "You're not winning this one," he snarled.

The crowd gasped, and I felt myself being pulled off Richard and taken to the ground because Drake had jumped off Vincent and pulled me down. Richard turned, picked me up, and crossed the finishing line.

"Well done, Rich... " I didn't even get to finish my sentence. He immediately dropped me on the ground and sprinted straight into the cake, literally *into* the cake.

The judges came over to award him the trophy, but he was only interested in devouring the cake.

That day, a legend was born. The legend of the boy who managed to finish a race in record time, as well as that same boy devouring a whole cake—all by himself.

On a side note, it seemed like the teachers had figured out what Drake had been doing, and he got into a lot of trouble.

Although I didn't get any cake, I was delighted by the results. Sparta came over and gave me a massive hug. "Well done, kiddo. I'm so proud of you. I'm sorry as well. I didn't realize that Drake had been sabotaging your equipment all day. That's why you didn't come first in everything else."

"Well, even if the equipment was fine, I probably wouldn't have come first anyway," I responded.

"Nice joke. I'm already looking forward to the next sports day. But I still think there is room for improvement, so you will join me on my three hours jog every morning."

I fell to the ground, completely exhausted.

Chapter 4

After the sports day, classes resumed as usual. Mr. Joy announced, "Great news, everyone. The school camping theme park trip is coming up. We have about two weeks left, so it would be wise if you all began packing your camping gear."

During dinner, I asked my parents about getting the camping equipment.

Immediately, my dad eagerly stood up with his hand in the air.

"Me! Me! Me! I'll go."

My mother just looked at him and sighed.

"Okay, so who else would like to come?" my dad exclaimed while eagerly scanning the room.

My older brothers and sisters vigorously shook their heads. I'd never seen them so terrified. Ani and Genie were about to put their hands up, but the twins grabbed their hands and forced them back down. "You'll thank us for this later," they whispered.

"How about you come as well?" my dad asked Genie.

"It's fine, it's fine. Don't worry, Dad. She'll be playing with me tomorrow," Finn said while covering our little sister's mouth.

"Okay, then, looks like just you and I are going this weekend," my dad said after he returned. "Be ready by 5 o'clock in the morning."

"5 o'clock?" I asked in disbelief.

For some reason, my older brothers and sisters were looking at me with pity.

We set off at 5 in the morning the following day, but it took us almost three hours to get to the shopping mall.

My dad was really looking forward to coming here

"Dad, why did we drive halfway across the country to come here?"

"Only the best equipment for my son."

That's nice, I thought.

"Not to mention, there's a lot of things I want to buy for myself too."

"Alright, Dad, here's the list. Let's get cracking," I passed it to my dad.

"Yes, yes," he muttered distractedly. "But first, let's head to that shop over there."

I should probably mention that Diya took me aside the night before and told me, "Whatever happens, don't let Dad go into a DIY store."

"Why?"

"Just trust me." She sounded serious.

So, he went inside and started looking around. I wasn't interested in most of the stuff, so I just kept following my dad. He seemed distracted by every little thing. But then I saw something that had been in my fantasies ever since I was a kid: night vision goggles, more famously known as Nitro 3000X.

Making up scenarios where these would be useful

I'd already spoken to my dad before we arrived here. My parents have a complicated rewards and punishments point system.

Thanks to joining the cooking club, coming first place in the race, and general good actions, I had earned enough points to buy something.

I grabbed the Nitro 3000x, ready to show my dad, but when I looked around, he seemed to have disappeared. As I was roaming the shop looking for him, a man that looked like he'd come from the Victorian era came into my view. He wore a long top hat, a suit, a long cane, and a long beard. Behind him was a small hyperactive young child. He reminded me of the preschool kids. The ones that look as if they've just eaten 100 chocolate bars.

The man walked past me and asked the person at the counter. "How do you do?" He spoke with a very posh tone. "Please, can I have that? What do they call it again?"

The young boy piped up, "Nitro 3000X! Nitro 3000X!"

"Yes, that. Can I have that, please?"

"Sorry, sir, but that was our last one."

He turned around to look at me and gave me a little nod.

The boy looked very upset as he came over to me. I thought he was going to start screaming for the night vision goggles. But instead, he offered me his hand, expecting a handshake.

I shook the young boy's hand, and the boy announced, "Well done, well done, you beat me to it. As a gentleman, I must accept my defeat with dignity." The older man looked incredibly proud of him.

The boy looked like he was about to burst into tears but was holding them back.

I sighed. "Actually, you can have this."

The boy was thrilled as he accepted the goggles. "That is very kind of you."

The old man bent over and whispered, "My name is Uno. I'm a man who pays back my debts. One day, I'll make sure to repay you for this."

"Ah, thank you," I said and left.

Although I felt slightly sad, I suppose remembering how happy the kid became was worth giving up the goggles. But I wondered, how was that man planning on repaying me? He didn't even take down my details. Oh well, onto more important things.

Oh, my goodness, what is my dad doing? He was leaving the DIY shop with what looked like half the store.

He had so much stuff, yet weirdly, none of it looked like it could be used for camping. I could see boxes of hammers and pliers, two vacuum cleaners, carpets, new floorboards, and who knew what else.

"Dad, don't you think you bought too much stuff? Don't we need to buy the camping things?"

"Don't worry, don't worry, you can never have too many drill bits, screws, and screwdrivers. You never know when they can come in handy."

And so, the same thing happened in every shop. We entered more DIY, clothes, shoes, and card shops.

"Listen, son. You can never have too many greeting cards."

My dad bought so many things. Funnily enough, none were related to camping, unless I was expected to make my tent out of T-shirts, screwdrivers, and "Congratulations on your baby" cards.

Eventually, my dad noticed that I was tired. "Weren't you going to buy a toy for yourself?"

Having failed to buy the night vision goggles, I re-entered the toy shop to buy something else. The shopkeeper pulled down a large poster for the famous Rocky Bouncing Balls.

"Can I buy a Rocky Ball, please?" I asked the shopkeeper.

He looked like he was going to cry. "Are you sure you want one?"

"Yes, please."

The shopkeeper sighed and went around the back. He returned with a tray full of these balls and took one out delicately, wearing gloves and a mask as if he were dealing with a dangerous chemical.

He was about to pass one to me when a young child came out of nowhere and knocked him over, spilling the balls everywhere.

The shopkeeper screamed, "No, not again!"

The balls bounced left and right, and up and down across the toy shop, leaving behind a path of destruction.

Eventually, they landed in a pile of teddy bears.

"That's it. I've had it. I'm never selling these again. These are even worse than the glass tennis rackets. I've lost so much money."

The shopkeeper turned to me, "Look, do you want the rest of these? I never want to see them again."

The tray was full of these balls. There were about ten of them left.

"I don't think I can afford that many," I said.

"No, it's fine. Take them for free. Just take them and never let me see them again."

Dear reader, these rocky balls will come in handy in the future. Well, to be exact, in the next book. But you will need to wait for that.

After ten minutes of searching for my dad, I eventually found him. He was walking along the shops, followed by the shopkeeper, who was pulling along a massive trailer.

Looks like Dad found himself a helper.

"I'm done, Dad. I only need to buy my camping things."

"There are several other things we need to buy first!" he exclaimed.

"Dad, I don't think there's much time left," I responded, concerned that the shops might shut down soon.

"We have plenty of time," he assured. At that moment, his phone rang. His face lost all happiness, and he looked like a ghost.

"Hello," he answered nervously. I couldn't hear what was being said. But he looked terrified. There's usually one person who could make my dad look like this: my mom.

Dad put the phone down and looked at me. "Um, yes, we should start the camping shopping. Maybe I did get a bit carried away."

Soon an announcement came: "Please note the building will close in ten minutes. Ten minutes."

"Oh, there's no way we can buy all this stuff in ten minutes, Dad. It looks like we have to come back tomorrow."

My dad was doing some strange stretches. You know, the ones athletes do before a race.

"Do you know what will happen if we don't get the camping equipment today?" Dad asked.

"No," I replied.

"Wifey, I mean, your mother is going to be incredibly angry with me. Very, very, very angry. So, let's get started," dad explained.

He turned to the shopkeeper.

"Please look after all this equipment, dear shopkeeper," my dad requested.

"Huh? What? I don't think I'm getting paid for this," the shopkeeper complained.

"Let's go, son," my dad commanded, and he began running.

I never knew my dad could move so fast. We sprinted through every shop, picking up all sorts of camping equipment within a few minutes.

The shoppers must have been wondering what on earth was going on—a grown adult man with a child was rushing through the entire place like their lives depended on it.

Somehow, ten minutes later, we returned and collapsed on the floor, completely out of breath.

We were sweating and completely exhausted. We had bought most of the camping stuff in under ten minutes, but I felt like I was going to faint. I was panting, sweating, and completely exhausted

"So, son, do you want to come shopping next week?"

Chapter 5

The following day, my body was aching from all that rushing around. We were told that there would be some important announcements in class this morning. I definitely couldn't be late today.

Just as I was about to head off, I noticed baby Bobby looking at me strangely and making strange sounds, and no one was around him. I rushed at the opportunity.

"Say, David, David."

As I attempted to coerce the baby into saying his first word, the baby filled his diaper with gunk instead. I could smell it, and so could everybody else.

"Right, so, everybody, I need to head out now. I'm going to be late for school," I announced, trying to excuse myself.

"Oh, no, you don't," said Diya grabbing my shoulders. "You were the last person to play with the baby, so you must clean him up."

"Who came up with this rule," I grumbled.

"Rules are rules. Why do you think no one was around the baby at this time?" added Sparta.

"Yes, everybody knows that at this time, baby Bobby fills his diaper, so no one goes near him," Genie chimed in.

So I reluctantly cleaned baby Bobby.

Soon after, I hurried to school. Upon arriving, I saw it wasn't Mr. Joy in front but Mr. Scowl.

He had a horrible smirk that told me that I was going to be in a lot trouble.

"Mr. Dexter, you're late," he remarked. "You'll be in detention during lunchtime."

"But the clock on the wall says I'm seven minutes early."

"Well, not according to my watch. According to my watch, you're five minutes late."

I sat down, knowing that there was no point in arguing.

Richard patted my shoulder. "Don't worry."

Soon after, Drake came in and apologized for his tardiness.

"Oh, no worries, the clock on the wall says you're on time." Mr. Scowl said with a horrible smile.

My mouth dropped wide open. This was so unfair. Mr. Joy soon rushed in, out of breath and red in the face.

"Okay, everybody, we just had a staff meeting," Mr. Joy explained. "The principal has made an incredible proposal. We will get new equipment if we raise enough money during the school fair. I'm sure everyone here realizes how important this is."

The sports guys cheered.

"Hopefully, the computers will get an upgrade," the clever kids cheered.

"And we will get an official room for the school newsletter club," the gossip kids cheered.

Class fantasy of new equipment

"Our class has been tasked with advertising, so we will make about twenty posters. We must do a good job with this, or people won't attend the fair. So, everybody, split into groups, and let's get started." Our group had me, Isaac, Richard, Cashy, and the class monitor.

"I can't believe they're making us do this silly work," complained Cashy. "I should call my dad, and he could pay the principal instead."

Cashy's dad was a wealthy businessman. His dad didn't want to send him to a private school. Instead, he wanted to send him to a 'normal people school' like ours, as Cashy puts it, so he could learn the 'normal ways' and not be a spoiled child.

So, we started but soon realized there was hardly any equipment to do the posters with.

We were given these huge banners that would be used as advertisements to post around town.

"Oh, sorry, I forgot to mention," said Mr. Joy. "Our art supplies are currently extremely limited, so the principal has instructed everyone to bring in most of the art equipment on their own. So you see, this is your way of giving back to the school."

We all looked at each other. This was typical of the principal. Today, we had just enough crayons to start on a little corner of the poster.

Over the next few weeks, we brought art supplies from home and spent most of the day working on our posters. The principal allotted two weeks of reduced study. I've never done so much painting before. My mom wasn't particularly thrilled, either.

"How are you getting so much paint on your clothes every single day?"

I was basically coming home multi-colored.

Nothing particularly eventful happened at home during this time, except the twins getting awfully sick after finishing all the animal food for Ani's pets.

"You monsters! How could you?" she screamed.

"Aren't you worried if we're dying?" they said after returning from the doctors.

"Are you dying?" she asked, sounding worried.

"No."

The weather was getting chilly. My mom gave us winter supplies, including a special knitted hat, scarf, and gloves. I am well known for these, as my mom makes them by hand.

And so, finally, after two weeks, our posters were finished. They didn't look too bad. However, someone muttered, "Enjoy it while it lasts." I looked back, and it was Drake. He had a nasty smile on his face.

The principal came in on the day we finished to look around and inspect the posters. When he came to ours, he concluded, "Not bad. Not bad at all." If I'm honest, this was mostly thanks to Cashy.

Surprisingly, it seems like Cashy had discovered a new hobby and had been doing artwork at home. Before this, he never seemed to enjoy anything unless one of his servants did it for him.

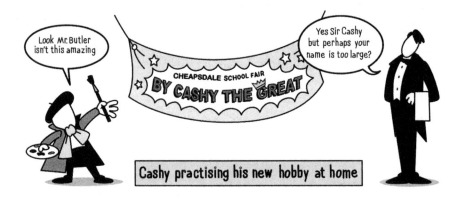

Cashy practising his new hobby at home

We headed out for our lunch break, feeling quite satisfied with the posters. I'm not the sportiest person, but we found ourselves next to the boys playing football (or soccer, as some call it) for some reason. I usually stood around talking to Richard and Isaac, maybe kicking the ball when it came to me. We were known by the sporty kids as legendary defenders. The reality was we were too lazy to move.

I suddenly heard a bizarre noise. Mr. Joy roared across the playground. It was like the whole playground became silent at once. We'd never heard Mr. Joy so angry before. Worst of all, he was calling my name.

"David Dexter, come here now!"

I felt like all the eyes were on me.

"What did you do?" Isaac asked.

"I don't know."

I was racking my brain, thinking about what I did or didn't do.

My legs felt like they were jelly as I walked across the playground. Mr. Joy had his arms crossed. "Follow me."

He took me to the classroom and showed me a strange, horrific sight.

The twenty posters had been completely covered in black paint.

Scene of the crime

"Please explain yourself," Mr. Joy demanded.

"But I didn't do this," I pleaded.

"Yes, I would have liked to have thought so. However, look closer at the posters."

Written at various points: "David was here."

"We also found this," Mr. Joy continued.

To my horror, my special gloves, hat, and scarf were clearly covered in bits of black paint.

For once, I didn't wear them out for the lunch break because the temperature was slightly warmer than usual.

"But why would I do this?" I tried to argue.

"That's what I would like to know as well," growled a voice. It was the principal, with Mr. Scowl following right behind him. This was the happiest I had ever seen Mr. Scowl.

"I'm really disappointed in you. All the evidence is pointing toward you. You will have to face the consequences. This is a real blow to the school. We can't afford another two weeks spent on posters because of the children's education, and we needed the posters for advertisement. Thanks to you, the school's fair could fall apart."

My mouth fell open, and I felt like I wanted to cry. "But I'm innocent."

"I'm afraid we can't believe that. And as a result, you will be banned from the school trip, and we will have to call your parents."

"And detention," whispered Mr. Scowl to the principal.

"Oh yes, and detention," added the principal. "Lots of it."

Soon after, the bell rang, and the class started filing in. They all heard the principal and Mr. Joy shouting from the playground. They looked straight at me and then back to the black posters.

It wasn't long before the entire class figured out what had happened.

While standing near my desk, Drake walked past and mocked, "You bad child, how could you ruin everyone's hard work." I was at breaking point and wanted to lash out at Drake. But instead, a piece of paper landed on my desk, which I quickly opened. "Do not get angry. Do not get angry. Do not get angry." Then, after sitting down, I gave Elder a nod to say thanks.

By the end of the day, news had spread to most of the school. On my way home, some kids threw garbage at me and shouted insults. That day was probably the fastest I had ever run home. That afternoon, my parents screamed at me while I tried to protest, assuring them that it wasn't me!

The journey home

"Are you honestly telling the truth?" my mum asked eventually.

"Yes, of course," I said.

"We believe you," my dad said with a smile. Their attitude changed quickly.

"Do you think your own parents wouldn't believe you? We wanted to hear your version first and also so that we could tell the school that we gave you a good telling off."

"But son, you've got to prove your innocence," my mum added.

Feeling slightly more cheerful, I walked upstairs, and one of the twins and Sparta were trying to teach my baby brother his first words.

"Say treadmill. Say treadmill."

"What's the point of teaching him that? He can't even walk yet!" Finn yelled. "This is how you do it. Say burger, burger."

"How is that better? He's only allowed milk and mashed-up bananas!"

I left them to it, not understanding why baby Bobby would need to know either of those words.

Genie, the genius, called me, "David, David, come here," while sticking her head out of the room.

Every room in the Dexter house was quite different. For example, this room was shared between Genie and Ani. Half the room looked like a farm, filled with different animals. The other side was sparkling clean with weird gizmos that my genius sister likes to work with. She wasn't facing me when I walked in.

"Ah, welcome to my office," she welcomed, twirling around on the spot. She had Ani's cat in her hand, stroking her like an evil villain. "So, I hear—" At this point, her speech was interrupted by the appearance of a few frogs jumping over onto her side.

"Ani, get these frogs off my desk! Look, they're making a mess. This is delicate equipment, you know?"

I do wonder how my sister gets all this weird scientific equipment. It must cost a fortune.

"So, I hear you are in a lot of trouble," she continued. "Now, the best thing to do here is gather evidence. Concrete evidence. No one will take your word for it except mom and dad. So, I think you might want to use some of these."

She pressed the button underneath her desk and out popped a whiteboard—flipped around—revealing an assortment of weird gizmos.

Frankly, some of them looked pretty dangerous.

"What, where, when... " I stuttered in shock. "How on Earth did you build this? Not just the gadgets, but how did you make the wall flip over?"

"No questions."

"Thanks, Genie, but I'm sure I'll get into more trouble if the school sees me with some of these things," I said whilst looking at her dangerous gadgets. Genie wasn't pleased.

The following day in class, everyone was glaring at me, clearly still annoyed because of the posters.

Isaac and Richard looked quite concerned.

"What are you going to do about this?" Richard asked.

"I think I know just the people." I needed an actual detective to come in and help prove my innocence. I couldn't get one, but I did have the next best thing.

At break time, we set out toward the "gossip" corner. This was where Snoop and his friends spent all their time. They write for the local school newspaper, and they seem to know everything that goes on at the school, from which children still suck their thumbs all the way to what the principal is having for lunch. But, of course, the leader of this group was Snoop.

"Oh, look who it is," taunted one of them. "Have you come here to destroy more posters?"

"Well, if you guys really know all the news in the school, you would know that it wasn't me."

The gossip kids become silent. It was very embarrassing for them not to know the correct news.

"Now, now, everybody, calm down," Snoop said. "You three, step into my office." It wasn't an office, just one of the benches on the side, but no one else was there.

"Right, Snoop, can you—" I began, but Snoop cut in.

"Let me guess, you approached me because you need evidence to figure out who ruined the posters, and no one believes you?"

"Yes," I replied, thinking I'd just found the right man for the job.

"I must warn you. My fees are not cheap."

"How much do you need?"

"I expect one chocolate, one doughnut, and one croissant every day."

Although this was less expensive than I expected, I was unsure how to get those.

"Don't worry," Richard assured me, "I'll cover that. In fact, if you do a good job, I'll give you a bonus."

"Really?" Snoop asked Richard.

"Really."

They both shook hands.

"Thanks, Richard," I said.

The next day | The deal

"Now, you need the right equipment, and we need to look the part."

We all stared at each other. It seems like Snoop was getting too involved in this detective stuff.

That afternoon, I approached Genie. "It looks like I will need some of that fancy tech stuff."

"Finally, my genius is appreciated," she rejoiced.

"What do you need? Laser beam? Plasma gun?"

"No."

"The P500 Electric scooter?"

"No."

"What do you need then?" Genie asked.

"Coat, glasses, and a magnifying glass," I said.

"What?" Genie stated, not amused that I was choosing a magnifying glass over her fancy gadgets.

So, the next day, I brought all the stuff to school and gave it to Snoop at break time.

"Excellent, excellent." He beamed. "Now, let's begin with giving you some lessons on detection."

"Huh?" I asked. "Why do you need to give us that?"

"Oh, so you're the experts, are you?" Snoop barked.

Richard, Isaac, and I looked at each other and relented.

"Fine, fine, sorry. Yes, please give us lessons."

Snoop's detective training

So, he made us do all these weird activities, look for daisies, and search trash cans.

"Now, when it comes to sneaking around corners, a good tip is to use your mirror."

"Now, remember, clues can be found anywhere. Suspect everything and everyone."

At one point, Isaac observed, "Oh look, someone dropped the chocolate bar."

Snoop ran over and tackled him to the floor.

"What are you doing?!" Isaac exclaimed, bewildered.

"Saving your life, that's what I'm doing. That could be planted by the enemy."

It carried on like this. "Right, I think you guys are ready. I'm very proud of you. I didn't think you'd make it through training."

By this point, we were covered in filthy bushes, doused in mud, and smelt awful.

"It seems that everyone is ready. Let's go investigate the crime scene."

We returned to our classroom during the lunch break. It was empty, but we saw the ruined posters in the corner. It was a sad sight.

"Everybody split up and start searching for clues," Snoop ordered. After about 10 minutes, Snoop said, "I've realized something very important," we turned to look at him expectantly.

"Whoever did this to the posters is not very nice." We sighed at the pointless information.

The next few days carried on like this. Every day we spent break times and lunchtimes searching high and low—not really being able to find anything.

"I don't think this is a good idea," Richard whispered as we wasted another lunchtime.

But one morning, Mr. Joy announced, "Attention everyone, Snoop has requested to show us a presentation."

And it seemed the principal would be coming to watch as well. What could this be for? I hadn't seen the principal since he punished me for the school trip. Snoop was standing in the front, pacing back and forth.

"I've gathered you all here today to prove David's innocence."

Snoop pressed a button, and a video started playing on the monitor. The whole class gasped. The video footage clearly showed Drake and his cronies getting black paint and painting all the posters. But who would have recorded this?

Snoop proving my innocence!

Mr. Scowl looked utterly appalled.

This may be only the second time I've seen Mr. Joy angry. It looked like the principal was going to say something, but Mr. Joy roared, "Not only did you ruin all our efforts, but you tried to blame somebody else!"

"May I?" the principal chimed in. "I'm afraid now it's your turn to be punished." Although I don't like getting others into trouble for no reason, this was well-deserved. The whole class was looking at me with apologetic faces.

Mr. Joy implored, "I think we all owe David an apology."

Everyone came and apologized—apart from Drake and his friends.

We all then rushed over to Snoop and gave him a big hug.

"How on Earth did you get that?"

"Oh, didn't I tell you my uncle is a security guard here? He recorded it."

We looked at him in surprise. "What? Why didn't you say this at the beginning? What was the point of getting all those inspector clothes and doing detective lessons?"

"Well, that was just a lot of good fun," he replied with a smile. Richard was about to say something, but I nudged him.

We looked at each other, shocked and tired but incredibly happy.

Looks like I was going to the theme park after all!

Chapter 6

Although the principal let me go to the theme park, he didn't hide the fact that he was still completely devastated. He thought the school's fate was doomed.

I didn't have too much time to worry about this. This was a hectic period of the year. Things became more serious in tone, our homework increased, clever kids went into overdrive, and our teachers wouldn't stop talking about our upcoming exams. Isaac was panicking.

"Isaac, we still have about two or three weeks till exams," I reassured him.

"Three weeks? Three weeks!" Isaac exclaimed. "Do you want to fail everything and become homeless? Now come on, take these. Both of you!"

Richard and I looked at each other. It was a revision timetable.

"Now hurry up. I don't want to see any slacking," demanded Isaac.

Isaac making our revision like a villain

Soon, Isaac—the nicest among us—became a monster. A clever monster who might eat you up if you didn't revise enough. I was utterly exhausted.

"Well, why do you think we wanted you to become friends with Isaac?" my mom said. She knew Isaac's mum for years.

Finally, after three weeks, it was the day of the exams, and the toilets were completely full. There were even queues formed outside. It seemed like everyone was really nervous. Mr. Joy let us into the classroom, and we had all our exam sheets spread out.

The school decided to have all the exams in one day to get them over and done with. By the end of the day, we were exhausted, but I thought my results might be okay. Maybe.

It was nearly time for the school theme park trip. I was feeling slightly nervous. It was going to be a three-day trip, and this was the first time I would be away from my family for this long. As it turned out, I wasn't the only one feeling a bit upset.

I returned home that day, and my mother was crying her eyes out.

"Mom, Mommy! Are you okay?"

"You're going. I might never see you again!" she cried.

"Don't worry, Mom, I'm only leaving for three days."

She started crying even more and ran off.

Kathy, the therapist sister, frowned at me, disappointed, saying that's not how you should calm people down. "Don't worry, the next three days are... " she started what would be a long lecture but couldn't finish. Then, tears began forming in her eyes, and she ran off.

Next, Mona called me into her room. She put her hand on my shoulder and said, "Look, don't worry about the stock market. Just relax. There's no need to get emotional. You're a big boy now... ." Again, the tears started rolling. Finally, she pushed me out of the room and shut the door.

"Look, man," began Sparta, "you've got to keep up your fitness, okay? You know, make sure you do ten thousand steps every morning."

"Well, I can't do that, but I'm going to miss you complaining about exercise."

By far, the best visit was from the twins. That day they were going for a French theme. After I walked into their room, they started crying without hesitation. However, they did say, "Look, we packed all our best food for you." Which was true.

They gave me some amazing French chocolates, snacks, and croissants. It was like the ultimate lunch box.

The following day most of the family was still crying. After Ani finished hugging me, I saw a long trail of snot left on my clothes.

"Now remember, when building a house, the most important thing is the foundations. So, you must let the cement set even if it takes a few days, okay? Do you understand?" sobbed Diya.

I didn't know why I'd need to know this, but I smiled and patted her on the shoulder.

After lots more tears and goodbyes, we were finally at school, waiting for the bus to collect us. The journey there was eventful. We had to stop about 100 times because most students needed to use the toilet. The biggest surprise was seeing three people I did not expect on the bus—Drake, Victor, and Vincent.

"I thought they weren't allowed to come?" whispered Isaac.

"Didn't you hear? Mr. Scowl requested that they come along," replied Richard.

"That's so unfair," Isaac protested.

What about when I wasn't allowed to come?

The theme park was one of the largest in the country, and we could see the roller coasters, drop towers, and giant wheels from a distance. Upon arrival, we saw a luxurious-looking hotel.

Arriving at the theme park

"Can we sleep there?" Bolt, the sporty kid, exclaimed.

"Sorry to burst your bubble, everyone," Mr. Joy responded. "We're not going to be staying in there. This is a camping trip. We will stay in the forest next to the theme park. Isn't it great being one with the great outdoors?"

"Why are we sleeping outside if there's a wonderful hotel?" asked Cashy.

"Because the school wants to save money, of course, it's expensive staying there," explained Mr. Joy. "But anybody who wants to go there is more than welcome."

None of us had brought much money, so the entire class stayed put. Well, nearly everyone; Cashy got up and almost ran to the hotel.

Soon a group of thirty kids started trying to make tents. I'm sure you can guess what the result was. Even after thirty minutes, it looked like a pile of pipes and cloth. Finally, after two hours of tears and help from the teachers, the tents were ready.

Then Mr. Joy announced, "Well done for building your tents. The theme park staff will now explain what will happen tomorrow." One of them looked slightly familiar—I wondered why.

"My colleagues will hand out the maps for you to follow. Each group must stick to its route. There will be a prize for whichever group visits the most rides!" explained one of the supervisors.

Everyone was ecstatic. However, I saw Drake walking past me and muttering, "Just you wait... I'll make sure to get payback for what you did to me."

Drake walked up to the staff leader, who looked remarkably similar to Drake. Soon they both turned and stared at me.

"Snoop, do you know who that person is?"

"Darwin, nineteen, a really nasty guy, has a big secret: he likes to sleep with a teddy called Cuddles."

"How on Earth do you know this?" I asked, amazed.

"Oh, and he's Drake's brother," he added casually. I had a bad feeling about this.

Drake plotting with his older brother and friends.

Our tent was shared by four people: me, Richard, Isaac, and Elder. Elder fell asleep immediately, but the rest of us were worried and couldn't sleep. Before long, we began hearing strange noises.

"Ooh... Get out of here!" It was a deep, frightening voice.

"What was that? What was that?" whimpered Isaac.

"It might be ghosts," Richard suggested.

"Be quiet," Isaac snapped. "Ghosts are scientifically impossible."

We could see strange outlines outside our tent, and these weird noises continued the voices of *'Oohs'* and *'Aahs'* and scary messages. The noises continued for a while, and soon we could see a shadow getting bigger and bigger and bigger. And soon, we could see the tent zip open from the outside. We were petrified.

"Alright, guys," Isaac sobbed. "If something ever happens to me, please auction off my robots to a museum. I don't want them to go to the recycling place."

"Yeah, if anything ever happens to me, please don't throw away all the moldy cakes I've got underneath my bed. Please give them to a museum as well," Richard sobbed.

We both looked at Richard. "We are not giving your dirty cakes to a museum."

Getting scared inside the tent.

Suddenly the tent burst open, and someone popped their head inside. It was a frightening mask. Three frightening masks! We all screamed at the top of our lungs. Elder woke up, and immediately, the masks disappeared.

We didn't know what to do, and we could see Mr. Joy through the opening in our tent.

"What's going on here?"

The three of us ran out of the tents, and Elder somehow fell back asleep. We could see the three figures which seemed to have masks on. We went straight to Mr. Joy.

"Um... um... these things! They're monsters!" Isaac wailed. "Monsters, I tell you!"

"I thought you didn't believe in monsters," Richard teased whilst shaking and holding onto Mr. Joy.

"You're just as scared as I am!" Isaac replied.

The things took their masks off. It was Drake's older brother and his friends. "Ah, we were going around giving out chocolates as a midnight treat. I don't know what's gotten into these kids."

"Oh, that's very kind of you," Mr. Joy beamed.

Our mouths opened in shock. "But... they were clearly... "

"No buts. It's not good to assume bad of people."

"Here, take your chocolate." They were the tiniest, most disgusting chocolates I'd ever tasted.

Some of the other children had come out of their tents as well. Some complained, "Seriously, guys, you better stop making so much noise." We went back into the tent. An hour later, something similar started, and we could see something dripping on our tent.

"Huh? That's blood! That's blood!" Richard exclaimed.

"That's not blood," Isaac said. "Why would that be blood?"

We could see red ooze coming all the way from outside our tent. But this time, it was different. We could hear screaming from other tents as well.

"No," I heard Drake's voice say. "Don't do it on anyone else's. Just these. We want these guys to panic."

"No, it's boring if it's just one tent."

I could hear arguing.

This time the lights really did come on from the outside. Mr. Joy had come out. "What's going on now?"

We rushed out of the tent again.

"The supervisors gave us food to share with everyone as a midnight treat," Drake said. This time they brought burgers, and it was clear the red stuff was just ketchup that they sprayed all over our tent.

My ketchup covered tent.

The kids whose tents the ketchup had fallen on, namely the gaming and gossiping kids, were not amused.

"This is ridiculous. They were clearly trying to terrify us."

"I don't know where they got these burgers from. They're rotten."

"Well, I'll have them if you don't want them," Richard suggested enthusiastically. Then, one by one, he ate everybody's burgers.

Bolt was staring at Richard devouring the burgers. "You've got quite the appetite, don't you?"

We crawled back into the tent, extremely agitated after all that had happened.

"This is ridiculous. They can't even let us enjoy a school trip," fumed Isaac. Richard nodded in agreement, and I looked at my watch.

The three of us couldn't sleep, still frustrated and angry, but we desperately wanted to sleep. Richard nudged Elder. "Hey, could you give me some advice to sleep?"

"Forgive everyone and sleep with a clean heart," he mumbled. Eventually, we all dozed off.

The activities the next day were disappointing. We were put into groups, and I was with Richard and Isaac. But our map was slightly different compared to everyone else. It directed us to only the rides with exceptionally long queues. By the time we got to the front, we were told:

"Sorry, you can't go on this ride. You need an adult with you."

"This is a special ride that you must pay extra for."

"You need to book 3 days in advance for this ride."

"But the map told us to go to all these rides," fumed Richard.

By the end of the day, we had not gone on a single ride. "This is absolutely ridiculous."

The sports kids were coming our way, and the head of them was Bolt. "This place is amazing! Did you try rock climbing?"

We said, "No. Look at our map."

"What!?" The sports kids looked at our map. "That's so unfair. Why were you allowed to go on all these rides?"

"We didn't. We just approached them, and they told us to go back."

Pretty soon, the clever kids arrived and quickly worked out what had happened. "It looks like you've been set up," they observed.

At the end of the day, we returned to the tent, exhausted and miserable. "Guys, I'm pretty sure the same thing will happen tomorrow. This is just so unfair. What are we going to do?"

Before I could answer, I noticed a note on my pillow:

Come to the ghost train.

"It says come to the ghost train."

Isaac blubbered, "This is probably some prank pulled by Drake. It's dark, and we shouldn't go at this time." It was about six o'clock in the evening. Almost everyone was back in their tents.

"But look, the note has the supervisor's signature. So we can say that we were told to go here," Richard insisted.

"Fine. I guess so."

So we headed toward the ghost train, and I was feeling quite tense. Everyone was back in their tents, and Mr. Joy and Mr. Scowl were nowhere to be seen. Eventually, we arrived at the ghost train ride, which was abandoned.

"Guys, this doesn't look like the right place. Maybe we should turn back," pleaded Isaac.

Richard speculated, "What's the point? We should find out why that note told us to come here and look, the cart is right there."

We squished into the little cart, and the ride began automatically. On a scary scale of one to ten, regular ghost trains are about a three or a four. They're not scary at all. But this one was about twenty. Someone had taken the scary factor up to the absolute max.

Weird monsters were popping out. We were sprayed with disgusting stuff that stank. However, after a while, the ride's speed increased, and I actually started to enjoy myself. Richard and I had our hands in the air. Unbeknownst to me, Drake was watching us through a camera.

"Urgh! He's actually enjoying this. Make it even scarier," Drake barked.

"He's not going to find it fun now," Drake's brother smirked.

More freaky monsters popped up. Finally, some of them even started touching the cart and throwing things.

"Oh, look, sweets!" Richard exclaimed. "Oh, I quite like these, actually." He even lifted his head up and started eating them.

Drake banged the screen that he was watching us from. "Why on Earth would you give them sweets?"

"Sorry."

Just when we really began to have fun, we heard a voice on the voiceover.

And what do you think you're doing?

We thought the voice was talking to us, but we could hear someone say, *"Sorry! Sorry!"*

The ride ended, and we were back where we had started. To our surprise, we could see the whole class outside in their night clothes and Mr. Scowl looking quite nervous. On the other side, I could see Drake, his brother Darwin and Darwin's friends. Behind them was a man I had never expected to see. It was Uno, the posh man in the stripy suit who I met at the toy store.

"Explain yourself," he demanded. Darwin didn't seem so frightening now.

"Uh… we were just trying to give them a fun ride," he mumbled.

"I see. And that's why you took them on this ride, which is strictly for adults?"

"Um… well… "

He was talking to Darwin and his friends. "Not only have you broken the theme park rules, but it has also come to my attention that you have given these young gentlemen this map."

For some reason, the man had the map that we were given.

"How did he get that?" I wondered.

"They clearly can't go on any of these rides. So why did you do this?"

"Um... um... sorry?"

It's funny how even the scariest of kids can sometimes seem so weak when adults tell them off. After dealing with them, the man began walking over to us.

"Well, I didn't expect to meet you like this," he said to me.

I looked up at him. "You are the man from the toy store!"

"After you helped me, I did say I would pay you back one day," he said. "I'm terribly sorry for this affair." He put his hands on my shoulder. "As a man, I must repay you for the kindness you showed my son. Is there anything I can do?"

I did have two ideas.

The stripy suit man was beginning to regret buying the goggles.

The next day we had a lot of fun. The entire theme park was reserved for us, so we didn't have to wait in queues. Nearly everyone was thrilled, and Isaac, Richard, and I were treated like heroes. Drake and his friends, however, had to spend the day in their tents. Drake's older brother and his friends had their duties changed slightly. We could see them doing unpleasant jobs as we went around the theme park.

"But one thing I don't get," Isaac wondered, "How did that man get our map?"

"Oh, I think I know. First, we should go and thank Snoop."

"Snoop?" the other two quizzed.

"Yes. He's the one who gave the stripy man the map."

Each of our parents had given us a bit of money, and we knew Snoop was obsessed with candy floss. So we all bought Snoop large boxes of candy floss and headed straight to him.

"Thanks for everything, Snoop."

"Ah, please. It was my pleasure. It's quite satisfying putting those guys in their places."

"But I am curious," Snoop said, "I remember you asking that tall man two things. What was the second one?"

"Ah, well, you'll find out tonight."

Later in the evening, the lights turned on, and many more visitors came.

"Whoa!" Snoop cried out. "That's very clever."

Mr. Joy was also quite surprised, and as we returned to the tents, we heard a faint voice saying, "You're an absolute genius! Absolute genius!"

"Who's saying that?"

Mr. Joy was coming our way, and it seemed like a voice was coming from his hand. We looked at it, and he was talking to the principal. It was a video call. "The principal would like a word with you," Mr. Joy said with a smile.

"Incredible work," he praised. "Really well done. You shall receive a special reward when you return to school."

It turned out that the man in the stripy suit was the theme park manager. I had requested him to put up lights everywhere advertising the school fair.

"COME TO THE CHEAPSDALE SCHOOL FAIR!"

The advertisement had more details about the date and location, and of course, thousands and thousands of people saw it.

Chapter 7

The following week went by in a flash, and before we knew it, it was the day of the school fair. The school had never had anything like this in its history. Thousands of people from all over the country came to visit.

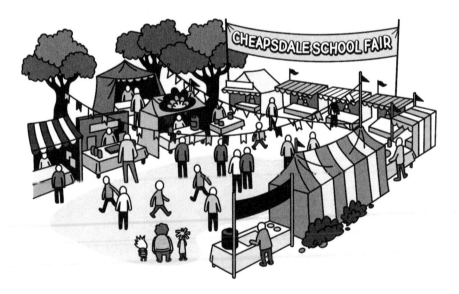

Thankfully, my family was able to make it too. We were given our own little space. The principal was treating me and my family like VIPs. He kept shaking my dad's hand, saying, "You must be so proud of your son."

"Yes," he beamed, "I am really proud."

There were lots of stalls such as dunk your teacher, dad races, and fish for a prize, not to mention a large variety of food stands. There were also people selling things.

"Dad, I don't need these chemicals anymore," Genie noted.

"That's lovely, but if the school finds out you've got these dangerous chemicals, we're probably going to jail. I don't even know where you got these from."

"Oh... right. Okay, never mind."

And still, everyone was trying to get my baby brother to say his first word. Mona had been very proud of herself.

"Well," she said, putting her arm around my neck. "Well done, little David. I've taught you well, haven't I? It seems you've truly understood the importance of advertisement in business. Let me tell you about the first time... ."

"Hey, let the kid breathe, man. He doesn't need to know your financial history," Sparta laughed.

"I suppose so."

And soon after, a massive man came waddling over. "Hello, David," he gushed, "I wanted to come and meet your papa."

"Oh, right. Gusto, here's my dad."

"Gusto! The famous chef? It's a privilege!" my dad exclaimed.

"No, you are the one I should be grateful to meet," the French chef beamed. "You taught your son some marvelous recipes." Then, he pulled out one of my most disgusting-looking sandwiches. "You must be so proud."

"Uh... " my dad looked disgusted at that sandwich, "Yes, very proud."

Apart from that, the day was a bit of a success, and the school made a lot of money. We found out that we would be getting a lot of new equipment. Everyone was delighted except for Drake and his friends, who had gotten into a lot of trouble after the theme park fiasco.

Toward the end of the day, we could hear the principal's voice ringing from the speakers. "I'd like to thank everyone for coming today. And a special thanks to David Dexter for arranging the great advertisement at the theme park. Were it not for that, I'm sure many of you would not have heard about this."

Before I knew it, I had many kids rushing over kids from my class and some of the older years, shouting, "David! David!" and throwing me into the air.

Baby Bobby was watching. Some of my siblings were still trying to make him say his first words.

"David! ... David!" the crowd was shouting.

"Come on, Bobby, say screwdriver," Diya persuaded. My family was still staring at him intently.

"Davi... " said the baby.

"No!" cried my family.

Did you enjoy book 1?
Visit adamwafi.com for news and
exclusive content

Did you enjoy book 1?
Visit adamwafi.com for news and
exclusive content

Did you enjoy book 1?
Visit adamwafi.com for news and
exclusive content